Anonymous

Ruth

A Song in the Desert

Anonymous

Ruth
A Song in the Desert

ISBN/EAN: 9783337191115

Printed in Europe, USA, Canada, Australia, Japan

Cover: Foto ©Andreas Hilbeck / pixelio.de

More available books at **www.hansebooks.com**

RUTH:

A

SONG IN THE DESERT.

"There, hand in hand, firm-linked at last,
And heart to heart enfolded all,
We'll smile upon the troubled past,
And wonder why we wept at all."

BOSTON:
GOULD AND LINCOLN,
WASHINGTON STREET.
1864.

NOTE.

THE writer hopes, by this little narrative, to reach a few of her sisters in sorrow. If to some it should seem to fall below the key-note of Christian privilege, they will remember that there are many whose experience is not yet true to all she has said. It is of those she has thought. "Silver and gold have I none, but such as I have give I thee."

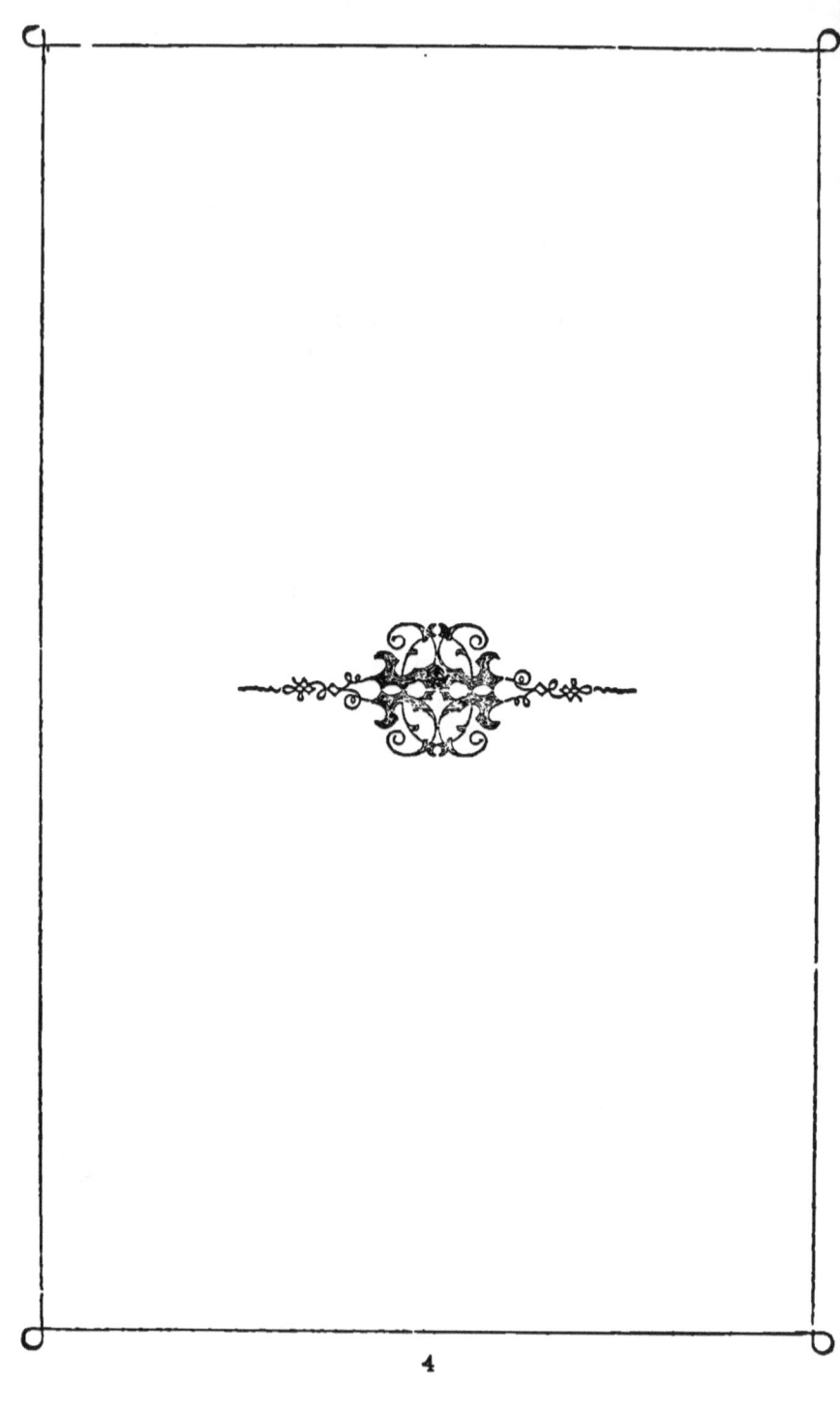

CONTENTS

A Song in the Desert.

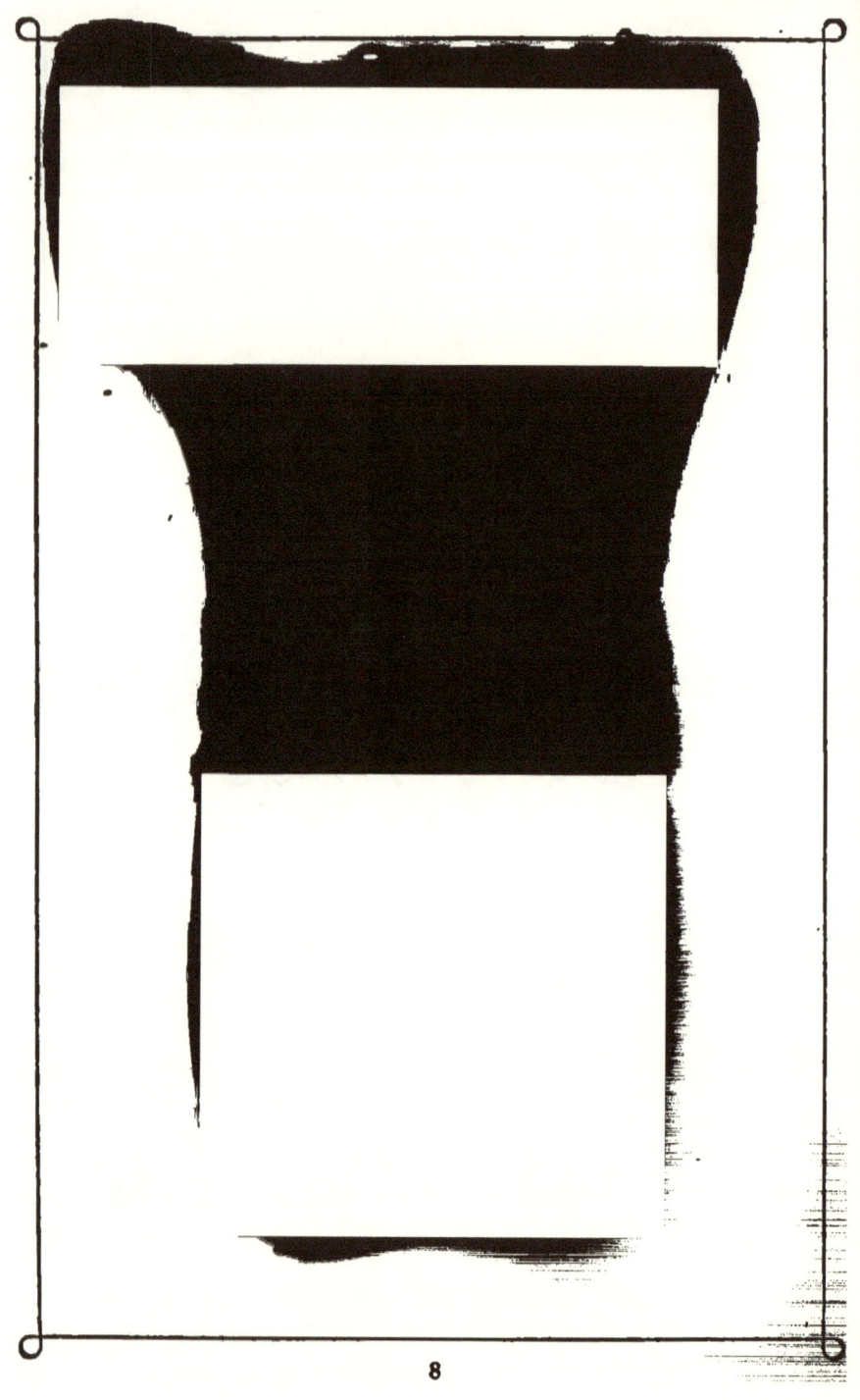

The Nightfall.

T was about an hour since they had told her, and she was now lying quite still, with her eyes closed and her hands tightly clenched on her breast. In the darkened room her face looked gray and death-like. She seemed scarcely to breathe.

"It is such a sudden blow," her sister

said, in a whisper; "it was only this afternoon she got one of his letters."

"Oh, Amy! it will kill her, — my poor child! Ruth, darling?" Her mother bent over the bed, with her hot tears falling like rain on the girl's dry, cold cheeks.

"Ruth, shall I pray?"

"Yes." The changed, chilled voice! it frightened them.

The mother thought words would freeze on her lips; but as she knelt, a prayer came to her, — was uttered for her, perhaps. She prayed as her dead husband might have prayed, with strong crying unto this sovereign God who had laid his hand heavily on her child — her eldest-born. She pleaded with the Christ who wept at Bethany, and who was no more here to bring back the dead whom he had taken utterly away. Would He not come near to this poor, crushed heart, which even her mother could not comfort now? Would He not tell her that the brave soldier had found rest with Him, where the shock of war, and "garments rolled in blood" should never be, — that all his pain had ended, — that it was for love of him and her that the great Captain had called him home? He who tempers the wind to the shorn lamb, would He not surely do as much for her child?

The voice which had tried to pray broke down in its faltering "Amen." Amy's sobs fell heavily on the air; but there came no moan nor cry from the pale lips which could yet frame no prayer of their own, — poor, quivering lips, which no warm kisses could ever more make glad. She unclosed her eyes at length, and turned with a child-like, helpless movement toward her mother.

"When was it? Tell me about it."

"It was day before yesterday; the battle was in the morning, — don't ask me, Ruth, darling, — don't! Wait till you can bear it better."

"I can bear it now. Did he, — did he live long after it?"

"No; his sufferings were very short."

"Can they, — will he come home?"

A long silence answered this question; then, —

"My poor, poor child! he cannot come."

A long shiver passed over her frame, but her anguished eyes did not flinch from asking one more question.

"There was no time for any message," was the reply.

Hearing this, she turned away so that they could not see her face.

"I would rather be alone," she said.

So they went, her mother stopping to give her a long, lingering kiss, to smooth her tangled hair, to feel the chill of her white face, to know that she could do nothing, nothing for her. She must leave her alone, — her child, her poor little Ruth, who had been all hers to love and help, since she came to her, a little wailing baby, so long ago. Now she must go away; she could not comfort her. She closed the door, and in the silence which fell on the dim room, Ruth was left alone.

To stand face to face with God who had smitten her, to feel sure of nothing in earth or heaven but his changeless will and her own consciousness of agony, — this belongs to those things which are "within the vail." She was alone with Him, — what avails it to say more?

After a while her mother came softly in and drew back the shutter. The green of the trees by the river-side, the sparkle of the waters, the shadows on the hills, and the broad line of gold in the evening sky, glowing and fading in its grand unrest, the flickering light down in the valley where the village children were at play, — this was what Ruth saw. The same world, was it? Did the light fall just so yesterday through the old, familiar trees? Did the happy river wind so among the meadows? Were those the voices and laughter of the little children whom she had known so long?

She closed her eyes with a long, low moan, and her mother, hearing it, drew the blinds again.

Presently Amy stole in with a cup of tea.

"*Please*, Ruth," — holding it to her lips.

Feeling its heat, she pushed it away, shivering; — *he* was so cold, so cold now, what had she to do with anything warm and life-giving?

"Amy, I can't, — I can't! Mother, you had better go now, — both of you, — the night has come."

The broken wail of her voice rang in her mother's ear for hours, and Amy sobbed herself to sleep. Ruth lay in her little room, with her hands still crossed on her breast, holding up a great prayer in their clasping, and her eyes wide-open to the darkness all night long.

They had been all to each other,—she and Frank. He had come to her in her sunny girlhood, making all her days a beautiful promise; she had not thought it *could* be broken,—had not God spoken it? And now he had gone from her,—had gone away utterly.

You know how she loved him; you need not words to tell you. By your own heart, too, you will measure her loss. She had been so happy, how could she bear it to wake from her dream, and know she should never more be glad? Hers had been such a trusting heart, it had clung so closely to him and his love, how could she stand alone, with all that had been her help lying mute and still by that far-off southern river? How could she come back to the wilderness of life, in which she could find henceforth no voice to answer her? How could she take up these weary hours and days which must make her future, remembering what they might have been, and how he would have blessed them and made them bright?

Her mother, going about the darkened home sorrowfully, in the days when Ruth would be alone in her still room, thought and prayed much over this in her anxious heart. What should she ask for her child? How could she, her mother, call her back to her desolate life?

The Conflict.

HE came among them at last, but she was not of them. Wherever she went, a shadow rested. The children shrank away, frightened at her black dress and white, changed face. Amy cried in secret over the sisters he had lost, and her mother's mute eyes followed tearfully her every motion. After a time, however, Ruth took up bravely her daily household cares and ministrations of love, interesting herself in the children's little joys and troubles, and teaching them all to find her warm kiss and helpful hand, even more loving and more patient than before.

Yet it was pitiful to see her, with her slow, sad step about the house, all the bright girl-look gone from her face; her eyes grown so large, and dark, and full of pain; her trembling lips trying to smile, — such a lonely smile it was! It was hard to hear the hopeless patience of her voice; to see how dully she looked out on the fields, all bright with the green shadows she used to love so, where

the dash of glad waters, the hush of pur-
ple hills and glowing sky and the tenderness of tremulous white clouds lay before
her as of old; and then to see her turn
away from them all as if they hurt her;
to see how her face paled when the twilight fell, and how she would steal quietly
away, — so quietly they would hardly
miss her, — and to know that the burden
of the day had grown so heavy, she could
no longer bear it.

The long months passed away, and
each one found her more patient, more
mindful of all thoughtful deeds and words
of love. She had long since taught her
lips to pray again; she thought she was

trying to make them frame the Abba Father of a life of suffering. She had taken hold of the hand of One who wept for her; she knew He loved her, she knew He would never leave her, she knew He had given her a life with which to glorify Him, — she *knew* it, but that was all.

If she had looked honestly into her heart, she would have seen that she was not taking it up *as* life, — not even for Him who spent long years of toil and suffering for her; she would have seen that she never once had lost the wish — I had almost said the persistent *will* — to die. Her recalled smiles and gayer words were only like perishing flowers which had root in the depth of this one ceaseless hope. Her friends looked on sorrowfully and felt that they were helpless, yet watched her with ceaseless prayer.

They had all been together one evening in the sitting-room, the children playing before the open fire, and Ruth and Amy shelling corn for them to parch. Their mother sat by, listening to the laughter of the little boys, and Amy's happy talk; but her ear caught most quickly the lowest of Ruth's quiet words, and her eyes fell oftenest and perhaps most lovingly on the little dark figure, with its pale face, and tender, helpful hands. She saw how happy the children were with her, how their arms clung about her neck when it came time to say "good-night," how she returned their warm kisses with a smile, and then, when they had left her, how her eyes saddened, looking dreamily into the fire, some faint, new pain seeming to creep into them.

"Ruth," said Amy, after a pause, "Sarah Greyson asked me, to-day, why you didn't come to see her as you used to, and if I didn't suppose you could do some district visiting down town with her this year."

Ruth compressed her lips, and her

hands twitched nervously, but she made no reply.

"And, Ruth, dear,—"

"Well?"

"You have never come back to your old place in the sewing-circle; and our reading-class ask me every week if we shan't see you again soon."

Ruth turned quickly, her face full of pain.

"I cannot, Amy; it hurts me so to go about among people. I'll help the poor in a quiet way; but a year is a long time to think about; and as for the reading, I do not care for that,—what use is it now?"

She turned her face again to the fire. Amy was silent, and soon rose to go up stairs, coming to kiss Ruth before she went.

"Amy, dear, I didn't mean to scold you, — you understand?"

"Oh, no, you never are cross to me or anybody; you're a perfect angel here at home, — only somehow, Ruth, — I don't know, — I wish —."

There was a puzzled look on her bright face. Ruth kissed it away with a laugh, and Amy left the room.

"Ruth," said her mother, after a long silence, "come up here and sit by me."

She came, sitting at her feet, her head

resting on her hand as if she were tired.

"Ruth, dear, you are doing everything you can for us at home, and I wonder at your gentleness and patience every hour; but, — don't think I am blaming you, my child, — but don't you suppose you could take up some of the work you used to love so, and mingle a little more with some of your old friends?"

"I cannot do it, mother, — I cannot go back to any more of the old life; it is all I can do to get along from day to day at home."

There was something sharp in her voice as she spoke.

"But, my child, there is One to help you; he will give you strength."

"He doesn't."

"Do you really *wish* Him to give it to you?"

"Why, yes; I wish to work for Him. What else have I left? I wish to work, if it might be short."

"You make no plans to do for Him, beyond a week or a month, my daughter. Why is this?"

"Because —. Mother, it's no use for us to talk about this; it only troubles you."

"Why is it, Ruth?"

"Because I cannot, *cannot* live!"

The firelight fell full on her face, so old and wan, with the lines on her forehead.

It would not take much more of this, her mother thought, to give her the rest she longed for. No home-ties could keep her, the love of the dear Christ himself only taught her to endure, and no more. What else remained? Who could help her child in this weary way?

"Ruth, what would Frank wish?" she said, at last. This seemed almost cruel, her lips quivered so, her hands clasped her mother's so helplessly, there was such a piteous entreaty in her stifled sobs.

Her mother's arms gathered her, as if

she had been indeed a little child. She could do nothing but love her; she must leave the rest with God.

"O mother! mother! *do* let me go!" and Ruth crept up to her with a little, low cry, as if the wind were wailing.

After a while she went up stairs and sat down in her room by the window. Amy was asleep, and it was quite still. She looked out to see the winter wind tossing the branches of the gaunt, leafless trees, and driving masses of cloud gloomily across the sky. In relief against the darkness, she could just see the outlines of the village church, and the low stone wall which bounded the cemetery

behind it. There her eye rested long-
ingly; there was quiet, there was repose;
to sleep there would be to find Frank.
She had no dearer love for all the bright
world now, than just that it held a little
space in which she could lie some day,
and be at rest, with the sweet breath of
violets and daisies and the melody of
singing birds above her. How had she
the strength to think that another year
might find her still away from Frank?
But, — if this were the will of God?

She was startled at the answer her
heart gave to this question. She had
thought herself submissive, — she had
thought herself resigned to his care.

The truth came suddenly to her. She saw how faint was her trust in his love, how feeble her best endeavors to serve Him in the lot He had appointed her, how utterly she did, in fact, rebel against his will, when that will decreed that she should live. She saw in herself the narrowed influence and dwarfed energies of a crushed, thankless life, taken only as a burden and borne as if she were a slave and not a child.

And why was this? Because God had taken away her treasure. But should He not do as He pleased with his own? Had He no more claim upon her love because one of his golden gifts had been recalled? And yet, — and yet how could she give it in the way He wished? With the persistence of grief, she came back to her old self-excusing. Would not her Master be satisfied if she did for Him all she could, from day to day? How could He ask her to accept a future into which Frank could never come?

The Vision.

OOKING out upon the clouds as if for an answer, she thought at last they moved and brightened, and a glory of light shone through them, turning the night to day. As she gazed, a form appeared therein, and moved toward her, a shining path growing before it, till it came to where she was. A sense of purity overwhelmed her, but she felt no fear. Looking up into the bright face above her, she saw why.

"Frank!" She waited breathlessly for his answer, gazing into his eyes, as if so she thought death might come to her. He smiled, — his old familiar smile it was, yet changed into something so perfect in its joy, that she wondered to see it. He called her by name, his voice like a strain of music that might wander forever about the Throne, yet tender still and full of human love. She stretched out her hands to him pleadingly.

"You have been sent to take me home, Frank?"

A change came over his face, a look

such as angels must wear in their *speech-less* moments, when, but for this mystery of angelhood, they might weep.

"It is not willed," he said; "you cannot come to me yet."

She bowed her head with a bitter cry. The voice from the cloud called her again.

"Ruth, *I* wish you to stay."

"*You* wish it?"

"His will is all mine now; I know no other."

"I cannot, cannot bear it, it is so long," she cried. His face seemed to grow dim as she spoke, his smile fading; she tried to touch his hand, but she could not reach it; he stood far away from her, the golden light about him deepening and glowing, as if it were the very whiteness of the Throne. And she seemed to know suddenly, though it was not his voice which told her, that so every hour of this hopeless murmuring placed more of distance between him and her. That even *he* should expect her to stay without him! —this was hardest of all. Hearing her sharp cry, he spoke again.

"I cannot so look on it, my poor Ruth; to us who have seen God, the life which he gives, even in its pain, must be thankfully accepted. I do not forget earth's anguish, or its love; louder than

all the music of our angel choirs, I have
heard your low moaning; but to see you
rebel against HIM, to see the love with
which his hand has separated us, and
then to see how you let it crush you, as
if it were a harsh and cruel thing, —
Ruth, all the pain that *can* enter heaven
is in my heart for you."

"Oh, Frank! what will you have me
do?" she wailed; — "take this bitter gift
from Him?"

"This *blessed* gift."

"Be *thankful* that I suffer?"

"That you suffer for Him."

"Take up these weary years as if they
were not filled with misery?"

"Take them with rejoicing because there is something yet to do for Him."

Seeing the great prayer for help on her lips, he drew near to her, his face brightening as if to bless her.

"My work was not finished," he said; "what I left undone on earth is given to you, to bring to God for us both. Will you do this for Him, Ruth? See —." Turning, he pointed to an opening in the clouds, where a long, lonely path stretched out before her; and looking, she saw that it was hers to tread. The way seemed to lead through a desert, but, as she observed it more closely, she saw that all along its sands homely duties, and kindly

words, and tender helps to the poor and
lowly, sprung and brightened like flowers,
and the joy of sad hearts whom she
should cheer was like the lull of foun-
tains in the parched air. Far in the distance a soul crossed her path, which, but
for her, could not be saved; and as she
listened to the dim sound of its blessings,
and looked eagerly forward, it might be,
perhaps, there were others whom God
had chosen her to bring to himself, — she
was not sure. A voice broke the stillness
of her long gazing.

"Your work and mine, — we will do it
together, Ruth." And, turning to answer
him, she saw, by the deathless love in his

eyes, that he would not leave her to toil alone. While she struggled with her tears for speech, the pure, bright face faded slowly from her sight. She stretched out her hands imploringly; she called his name; but his smile was her only answer. She awoke with a start, to find her dream had faded, and she sat alone by her window. Amy still slept soundly, and the room was cold and dark. Turning, with a sick sense of disappointment, to look out into the night, she saw that the clouds were breaking away, and in the bit of clear, still sky above her head, a single star shone like a smile.

The first whisper of possible peace she

had heard since Frank left her came, as she bowed her head, her lips moving as if in prayer.

The Daystar.

IT was only Ruth's clinging kiss on her mother's lips, and a smile bright with deepened love turned on Amy, which told them that in the watches of the night God had spoken to her a promise of better things, and sent Frank to help her.

But they looked at her in wonder, as every day she followed the voice which led her on, seeing how resolutely she tried to dispel the gloom that her grief had brought into their home, and how she struggled to recall in its stead some of her old playful ways, which were the charm of all their household memories. The dearness of her sister-love, which they had sadly thought was gone, as everthing else had gone which held her to the past, came back to gladden them, and they knew it truer, tenderer than before.

The little boys felt no longer that they must hush their noisy plays before the shade on her face, for a smile was there too, and they thought only of that.

Ruth liked to play with them and see them happy, and Ruth was so patient with them; Ruth made all hard tasks so easy; Ruth had such a pleasant way of settling their troubles; they had such talks with Ruth at twilight, after they had said their prayers, when she came up and sat down on their little bed!

The buoyancy of Amy's girlhood was no longer checked because of her sister's loss; she came, at last, to confide to her again all the joys and plans, which had never seemed half hers unless Ruth could share them.

"And as for mother," she would say, —"why, Ruth, I believe she lives by loving you." And Ruth, turning with her quiet smile, would see in her mother's eyes that which made her go up very softly to hide her face on her shoulder, and feel the caressing hand on her hair.

But it was not in her home alone that her patient heart drew the blessing of others to itself. There were old friendships to renew, and almost forgotten occupations to take up again for their sake. There were many, too, whom God had smitten, who knew Him not as a Comforter. These called to her, and her own suffering made her eye quick to find them.

So she went down among those who

were poor and despised of men, as her Master had gone before her, seeking the sorrowful ones whom she might help. At every step she met them. She had not known before how much unaided misery there was around her.

From their stifled factories and squalid homes, they came to her. She drew near to them to call them friends, and that with humbled heart, for grief had made desolate ways for them as for her, and the same Saviour who had been her Helper loved them.

She could tell you of discouragements which threatened to overcome her strength, of ingratitude where she had labored most and hoped most surely, of temptings to fall back into the selfish indolence of her grief, of hours when her struggles with the wish for death were bitter, of hours when the rod seemed sharper than she could bear.

But she would tell you, too, of a Help that always waited for her, of a Strength that gave her courage, of a Love that never forgot her.

She would tell you, with a faint flush on her cheek, and moistened eyes, that it was very little she could do; but perhaps that would be accepted, and some time she might see that her efforts had not been all unavailing. *Some time!* Her fingers would turn her betrothal ring unconsciously as she spoke, and you would know at once what she meant. But she was not to wait for this, to see the results of her work. Though we cannot know how brilliant the crown may be at last, some of its jewels will fall in our path as we walk.

She thought of this thankfully one night, when she had planned a festival for a crowd of little children, whom she had taught, in her patient way, for many months. They came from their dark, unwholesome homes to frolic under the trees and in the garden, — the same garden where she and Frank used to walk.

She thought, with a smile, how it would please him to see them there.

The little ones had brought their mothers and sisters with them, shyly, — sometimes a whole family, indeed; for, "didn't the lady ask 'em all to come; and Molly and brother Tom had a holiday, and thought they'd walk along, too; and didn't she want to see the baby, which couldn't come without mother, no-how, and could creep all round into everything since she saw it?" And the little thing would be sure to find its way over the soft grass to her knee, and she would take it up to kiss it and play with it, the proud mother standing by.

One neatly-dressed woman cast her keen eye over the lawn, to single out three or four rosy children from the group, and spoke suddenly, —

" To think," she said, putting her apron up awkwardly to her eyes, — " to think how them little things was used to be left without a morsel to eat all day long, in their miserable rags, and me lying drunk on the floor, or beatin' of 'em and thrashin' of 'em about, — poor innocents! — till they didn't know what mother meant, but a sort of devil! and then to see 'em so clean and tidy, and me so happy, and the rum-cupboard all cleaned out, and filled up with their little books and clothes; and to think how you come to me, when I was goin' to shut the door in your face, for I hated such like you, who was rich and good; and how you said, in that soft voice o' yourn, 'didn't I want somebody to help me bring up the little creeturs decent, and learn 'em how to love me, and, I— I— God bless you! I keep a chokin' and talkin' both at once, and make a fool of meself thinkin' on it all!"

While she stood there, hiding her rough face in her baby's neck, another voice joined with hers,— a slight woman she was, with a pale face and a mourning ribbon on her bonnet. She looked at the laughing baby with hungry eyes.

"Mine was so pretty!" she said, in a sort of appealing tone to Ruth; "just so, warn't he? And my heart was broke for him till I see you."

Ruth took her hand very quietly, with the quick tears in her eyes.

"You told me," said the woman, — "you told me where he'd gone to, and taught me the way to find him, and told me he'd wait for me, and love me, with his pretty ways, in heaven, just the same. Yes, he was a winsome baby, was my boy! I was just thinkin' how he'd have looked, with his red cheeks, tumblin' round among them little things, and comin' up to kiss you along with 'em."

Just then, a gentle pull at her dress caused Ruth to turn and see a pair of very sad childish eyes fixed on her, and to hear the story which had darkened them: "Father had drank up all the money, and mother was lying sick at home, and they hadn't no dinner all day; and would she mind her saving her supper, when it came time to eat, and carrying it home?—she wouldn't let nobody know, and would hide it right off quick in her pocket."

She had scarcely comforted the child, and brought back the light into its eyes, before Amy called her to start some merry game under the trees. With her smile ready for them in a moment, she turned away and joined the children's sport.

After that, a happy mother came to her, spelling out last week's letter from her soldier-boy, that Ruth might read and rejoice with her. Then it was a shy girl telling a story of her lover's long furlough, and how brave and good he was, and he wanted to see the lady; "would she mind dropping in, when she was down, to say a bit to him, or should she fetch him up to the house with her, some time after mill-hours were over?"

Close behind the blushing girl, another stood waiting to speak, — so close that she heard the happy talk, and turned away with a sudden motion like one in pain. It was not long before Ruth stood by her, looking into her face, pale with its stamp of early widowhood. What were Ignorance and Poverty that they should rise up between them now? In their kindred loss, Ruth thought, they met on common ground. She drew the girl's hand through her arm, and wandered down into the garden with her. There was little to say, — only a few kind words, and then to follow them by a silence in which the touch of the cool air, and the light among the flowers, might bring their own soothing to the tired heart.

So they came to her, one by one,— these neglected ones, into whose dark lives she had brought such brightness,— they came to bless her and go on their way rejoicing.

You would have wondered to see her passing among them, with the sunlight on her quiet face, and the smile on her lips, so patient she was and full of tenderness for them, so full of courage for their future, so earnest in her sympathy with their joys, so quick to divine where their troubles were and give them comfort.

The children, made happy by their plentiful supper, had grown tired with their sports, and gathered around her, rubbing their eyes with their little brown fists, to say good-night, — and at last she was left alone. She sat down under the trees where the birds were chirping sleepily over her head, to watch the group in the road, — the women hushing their babies to sleep as they walked; the happy children counting their store of apples and candy drowsily, and treading down the daisies; the young people stealing home, two by two, in the twilight, and a solitary figure, in a dark dress, lingering behind them all. That figure would turn again and again, to look at her, as she sat there alone, in the grey of the evening, as if it longed to come back and tell her how the broken hearts for which she cared prayed God to speak to her the same promise of peace she had spoken to them.

She watched the girl till her form grew dim in the dusky light, then, bending her head, listened for the last sound of the children's laughter.

When that had died away, she covered her face with her hands.

All these had blessed her, — had *blessed* her! Should she let their voices call to her in vain? Should she not thank God that she and Frank could so work together for Him?

One upon earth, indeed, and one in heaven, but never parted; and both his who gave them each to the other, she thought, and raised her eyes to the western hills, where the sky was clear. There was a prayer in their gaze that could not be uttered.

Amy came up with the children to say "good-night," and, taking their little hands in hers, she went slowly up to the house to find her mother.

With a fearless eye she looks now on her future, for she knows who has decreed its every moment in love. What it may be, — how long, how short, — belongs not to her care.

She sees in all the kindliness of daily life, a sweet incense which may rise to heaven like a prayer, and make her strong. All the thorns in her way she will press to her heavy heart and turn to flowers for his sake whose grief alone deserves such sharp crowning.

What if her steps do falter on this rough way? She knows her Saviour is there; she only asks to hear his voice, and she will go wherever it shall guide her. He will not ask of her too long a journey. He knows how she loves her soldier, and will, in his own good time, bring her to the home in which He waits for her.

So, hand in hand with Christ, she treads the Desert. She learns to gather, note by note, the broken harmony of her days. This is the burden of her song:—

"Here am I, Lord, and the Life which thou hast given me."

The End.

www.ingramcontent.com/pod-product-compliance
Lightning Source LLC
Chambersburg PA
CBHW031247260626
47169CB00007B/2483